and the
Amr Ants

by Rowaa El-Magazy

illustrated by Stevan Stratford

Note: This book uses the name Allah and God interchange...
One Eternal God, Lord and Creator of the Unive...

ﷺ *Sallallahualayhi wa sallam* means 'Allah's blessing and p...

السلام *Alaihis Salam* means 'Peace be upon hi...

D1064366

THE ISLAMIC FOUNDATION

It was a very hot afternoon.
Amr was sitting at the table, resting his
chin on his hands, his eyes staring at the
clock on the wall. Everything seemed to be
unusually slow today. It was as if time
stood still.

His father was late home from work
and Amr was very, very hungry.
The smell of the grilled chicken in the
oven made him feel even hungrier.
Suddenly Amr had a bright idea. Maybe his
mother would give him just a little
something to eat to ease his pangs of hunger!

"**C**an I have a biscuit, Mum? Please?" asked Amr, with
his hand over his stomach.

"Here, take this apple, but no biscuits before dinner!" laughed his mother.

"Why don't you take your eyes off that clock and go and play in the garden
and watch for Dad? Then you won't think so much about your stomach!"

"Good idea! *Jazaki Allahu Khaira* (May God give you many rewards!), Mum,"
said Amr biting happily into his apple. He gathered his marbles and headed for
the front garden.

He set up his marbles on a flat stone of the garden path, and settled down on
the grass to shoot. With his eyes close to the ground, he noticed an ant
struggling with a breadcrumb. Soon, a second ant met the
first and they seemed to whisper to each other, their
little feelers furiously waving back and forth.

Amr forgot his marbles and lay flat on the ground to watch. After their little chat, each ant went on its way. Then another ant arrived to help the first. Amr noticed a long line of busy ants working very hard at carrying more breadcrumbs.

"Where are they getting these crumbs from?" he thought. "There's no bread in the garden!" He followed the ants back to the house, up the wall, and to a crack beside the kitchen window. There was a line of ants going in, and another line of ants coming out. Amr went back to his spot on the grass. He had forgotten all about his hunger.

"Watching ants is more interesting than playing with marbles!" he thought to himself. He put his head down very close to the ground.

All of a sudden, someone wearing a large boot stepped close to Amr's hand and squashed some of the ants. Shocked, Amr looked up and saw the boy who lived down the road.

"Squashing ants is more fun than watching them!" said the boy with a big grin on his face. He then began to stamp on the line and carried on all the way up to the kitchen window.

Amr jumped up and shouted, "Stop it! That's cruel! How dare you kill these little creatures for no reason?"

"These little creatures, these poor, defenceless little creatures!" teased the boy, stamping and stamping with his big boots.

Amr could not stand it. He knew he should not fight without a good reason, but this seemed reason enough. He clenched his fists and prepared to attack, even though the other boy was taller and better built.

At this very moment, Amr's father arrived home from work. He jumped out of the car and stood between the two boys, who were all ready to start a fight.

"As-salamu alaykum (peace be upon you!). What's wrong, boys?" he asked calmly.

"He's squashing the little ants!" said Amr angrily.

"Oh, they're just ants!" said the boy. "He's making a big fuss about nothing," he added, shrugging his shoulders.

Amr's father looked at the boy. "Did anyone ever kick you?" he asked quietly. The boy looked surprised, but answered, "Yes, I get kicked in fights all the time."

"**D**o you enjoy being kicked?" asked Amr's father. "Would you like to be squashed underneath someone's boot?" he continued.

"Uh, no, not really," replied the boy.

"The ants don't like your boots either," remarked Amr's father. "Just because you're bigger, you have no right to hurt them.

Would you like to have dinner with us?"

"What? No, no thanks," said the boy, confused. "I'll be going now."

At that moment, Amr's mother called from the kitchen, "Food is ready. What's keeping you?"

"Are you sure you won't change your mind?" asked Amr's father, but the boy hurried away without saying a word.

The dinner table was ready and full of delicious food. Amr's father smiled and said, "*Alhamdu-lillah* (Praise be to God), it is really a great gift from Allah to come back from work and find a house to rest in and good food to eat." Then he looked kindly at Amr and his wife and added, "And it is a greater gift to have such a caring family!"

"*Bismillah ar-Rahman ar-Rahim* (in the name of God the Most Compassionate, the Most Merciful)" said Amr and his mother together, and they all began to eat. While they were enjoying the meal, Amr's mother asked, "What was happening out there? Why were you arguing with that boy, Amr?"

Amr explained. "That boy was squashing the poor little ants. Allah made the ants, same as He made us, and hurting them for no reason is nasty! Besides, I was having fun watching them. They're really interesting."

"**W**hy is that boy so rough?" resumed Amr.

"Well, he did say he gets kicked in fights, so he obviously is used to rough behaviour. He probably thinks that it is the only way to solve problems," explained his father.

"Yes, but these ants had done nothing to him."

"Sometimes, people use force even when it is not necessary, just because they feel strong and do not stop to think of the smaller and weaker ones," said Amr's mother, "it becomes like a second nature to them."

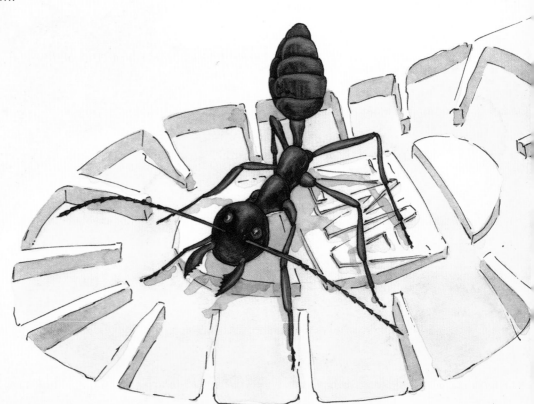

"**D**o you know the ants glorify
and praise Allah?"
Amr was surprised. "Ants praise
Allah? How?"
"Everything praises Allah," explained his father.
"Ants praise Him by doing what ants do. They
praise Him by doing their work perfectly. Do you remember
the story about Prophet Sulayman ﷺ and his big army?"
"Yes, yes, I remember!" exclaimed Amr, getting very excited. "He's the one
who could talk to the birds! And he could understand everything! And the
hoopoe gave him messages. But I don't remember about the ants exactly..."

"**P**rophet Sulayman ﷺ, liked to go out with his army. In the army he had jinn, men and birds," said his father.

"Did the birds have to walk?" interrupted Amr.

"Of course not," laughed his father, "they flew overhead in formation, like aeroplanes. One day the army was marching along and they were so many that the ground shook. They were passing through a valley where some ants lived. And, as you know, ants are so small we hardly notice them at all.

One of the ants, probably a guard, heard the army coming. It realized that the rest of the ants were in danger of being squashed unnoticed by the huge army. They were probably wearing huge boots," joked Amr's father.

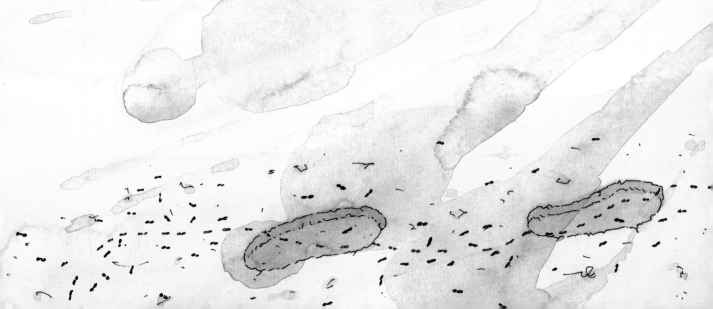

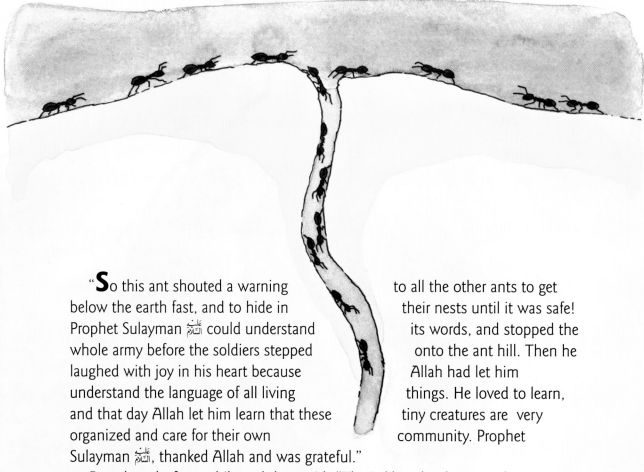

"**S**o this ant shouted a warning to all the other ants to get below the earth fast, and to hide in their nests until it was safe! Prophet Sulayman ﷺ could understand its words, and stopped the whole army before the soldiers stepped onto the ant hill. Then he laughed with joy in his heart because Allah had let him understand the language of all living things. He loved to learn, and that day Allah let him learn that these tiny creatures are very organized and care for their own community. Prophet Sulayman ﷺ, thanked Allah and was grateful."

Amr thought for a while and then said, "That's like what happened to me today. I never looked at ants before, then I learnt something and it made me happy. I'd like to learn more."

"Good," said his father. "Come with me!"

"*A*lhamdu-lillah (Praise be to God) for the food. Thanks, Mum!" said Amr, and he and his father went into the living room. His father pulled a new CD out of his briefcase and showed it to Amr.

"En..en..encyclo... what?" stuttered Amr.

"Encyclopaedia of Nature," read Mum, who had come in from the kitchen. "So that's why you were late home! You bought us a surprise *Jazaka Allahu Khaira!* (May God give you many rewards)."

"What is an en-cy-clo-what-d'you-call-it?" asked Amr.

"It's a book or CD that gives us information on all areas of knowledge", said his father. "We can look up whatever you like. But, first, do your homework! That's one way you can praise Allah. Did you know that?"

"**Y**es!" replied Amr. "I'm going to study very very hard and learn a lot of things, just like Prophet Sulayman ﷺ!"

"Peace be upon him," added his father, helping him with his school bag.

"*Inshallah!* (if God Wills)" said his mother. "Allah loves you to study and learn. If you need help with your homework, you'll find me in the kitchen."

So Amr studied hard and finished his work in time for the *Isha* prayer. After the *salat* (prayer), his father switched on the computer, and asked, "Which subject do you want to learn about, Amr? Let me guess..."

"Ants!" said Amr, very pleased. "Thanks, Dad!"

So up on the screen came a picture of an ant, and Amr and his father began to read.

"**A**nts live all over the world except in very cold places. There are over 10,000 different kinds of ants..."

"Masha Allah! (by God's Will!) Really!" exclaimed Amr.

"Shhh!" said his father, and carried on reading "Ants are social insects. They live together in nests with thousands of other ants. They are very organized. Each ant has its job to do. Each nest has one queen that spends its whole life laying eggs. There are worker ants who gather food and take care of the young ants in nurseries. There are soldier ants and guards that protect the nest and accompany the workers to protect them, too.

The nests have rooms and long halls. The ants dig them under stones or inside logs or underground.

There are different kinds of ants. There are leaf-cutting ants. Their soldiers have big jaws to cut the leaves into small pieces.

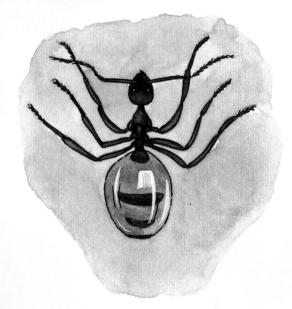

There are honey pot ants. They eat the nectar of plants. Some of the worker ants eat so much they swell up, and then they lie in the nest pouring out food when anyone wants to eat.

There are wood ants, that live in the woods, and can carry things much larger than themselves.

And the most amazing ants are army ants, that have no nests. They are on the move, marching... through the fields and woods and eating everything that gets in their way!

Ants are very important. They mix air into the soil by digging tunnels. This helps trees and other plants. They often kill harmful insects.

You can learn more about ants by keeping an ant farm and watching them every day."

Amr's father stopped the CD. Amr was very excited. "Dad, Dad, can we have an ant farm? Please, please?"

"Let's ask Mum!" replied his father. Amr went to ask his mother, who was in the kitchen washing up.

"Mum, Mum, can we have an ant farm? Please!"

"Okay, Amr, but only if you promise to take care of it and not let the ants die. That would be terrible!"

The next day
after school, Mum and
Amr went to the library
and found a book on
farming ants. Then they went
to the pet shop and bought an
ant farm and some ants to go in it.
Back home Amr set up the farm in the garden shed.

At first the ants did not know what to do. They crawled around on the glass and wandered here and there. Then one of them started to dig.

Others watched, and then began to help. Soon a small tunnel ran down into the earth. Amr watched, amazed. His mother had to call him three times to dinner. Immediately after dinner, Amr was back in the shed again, watching. His father came in.

"I've bought you a notebook," he said. "Scientists learn a lot by observing things and taking notes."

Amr thanked his father and during the next few days, Amr wrote a lot of notes. His mother helped him key them into the computer and he made a big report on ants as part of a school project. The report was a great success and several other children became interested in ants.

One day there was a knock at the shed door. It was the boy with the big boots from down the road. *"Assalamu Alaykum!* (Peace be upon you). Can I see your ants?" he asked.

"Wa Alaykum Assalam (and peace be upon you too). Yes. Come in," said Amr, holding the farm carefully in case the boy decided to kick it. But the boy only looked.

"Gosh! Look at those ants going down that tunnel!" he said. "And look at that one carrying that huge rock! How can it do that? It must be very, very strong!"

"By the way, what's your name?" asked Amr.

"Masud", replied the boy. "I know yours is Amr because I heard your mum call you many times before." They shook hands.

"I must tell you", continued Masud, "that your report on ants is great. My teacher read it to the class. "

"Thank you", answered Amr, beaming with joy. "You know, what you did to the ants really upset me the other day...", he added seriously.

"I am sorry", replied Masud. "I just did not realize that they are living creatures and that they care for each other and do such useful things."

Amr and his new friend watched the ants for a long time. Amr's mother watched them from the kitchen window and saw them studying the ants closely, then Amr taking notes in his little notebook. "Knowledge is the best gift one can ever have," she thought to herself. "Subhan-Allah (Glory be to God), we never know what the future will bring!"

She prepared dinner and called the boys: "Amr! Come straight away and bring your friend!" Amr introduced Masud.

"Masud, you are welcome to stay for dinner!" said Amr's mother, with a big smile on her face.

"Yes, with pleasure, thank you", replied Masud. "You'd better come in, then, and telephone your parents. Tell them we'll walk you back after dinner."

And this was how Amr and Masud began a long and close friendship, brought together by such tiny creatures as ants and... by the Will of Allah!

"Whoever seeks to gain knowledge, Allah shall make it easy for him to go to Paradise. For that person, the angels spread their wings, and all those living in the heavens and the earth, including the fish in the water and the ants in their nests, ask Allah for forgiveness for that person." (Hadith)